Women Inventors

3

Catherine Greene, Madame C. J. Walker,
Harriet Hosmer, Yvonne Brill,
Nancy Perkins

by Jean F. Blashfield

Capstone Press

MINNEAPOLIS

Printed in the United States of America.

Capstone Press • 2440 Fernbrook Lane • Minneapolis, MN 55447

Editorial Director   John Coughlan
Managing Editor   Tom Streissguth
Production Editor   James Stapleton
Book Design   Timothy Halldin
Picture Researcher   Athena Angelos

Library of Congress Cataloging-in-Publication Data

Blashfield, Jean F.
  Women inventors / by Jean F. Blashfield.
    p.   cm. -- (Capstone short biographies)
  Includes bibliographical references and index.
  Summary: Each volume presents brief accounts of five women and their inventions.
  ISBN 1-56065-276-4
  1. Women inventors--United States--Biography--Juvenile literature. 2. Inventions--United States--History--Juvenile literature. [1. Inventors. 2. Inventions. 3. Women--Biography.] I. Title. II. Series.
  T39.B53 1996
  609.2'273--dc20   95-442
  [B]   CIP
                                                                  AC

Table of Contents

1

2

3

4

5

6

7

8

COTTON GINNING AND CLEANING.

Catherine Greene
Too Much a Lady?
1755-1814

One of the most famous inventions in history is the cotton gin. This device removed the sticky seeds from the fluffy fruit, or **boll**, of the cotton plant. Before the cotton gin was invented, seeds had to be removed by hand.

When cotton could be cleaned of its seeds easily, plantation owners were eager to grow it. These owners used more and more slaves to grow the cotton. The cotton gin contributed to the growth of slavery and, eventually, to the American Civil War.

A 19th-century print shows the machines used to prepare cotton for the factory.

Where does a woman inventor come into this? Catherine Littlefield Greene was responsible for getting Eli Whitney to design the cotton gin. Everyone agrees on this fact. Whatever other role she played is debated by historians.

The General's Lady

Catherine Littlefield, called Caty, was born in 1755 on Block Island, off the coast of Rhode Island. She was married to Nathanael Greene, who served as a general under George Washington. After the Revolutionary War, Greene was granted an estate in Georgia, on the Savannah River.

The Greene family settled on a plantation called Mulberry Grove in 1785. Soon the general died, and Catherine found herself a widow with many debts to be paid.

Catherine met a young man named Eli Whitney, who had come to Georgia to work as a tutor on a neighboring estate. When the job fell through, she and her estate manager, Phineas Miller, suggested to Whitney that he could probably make some money by designing a device to remove the seeds from cotton bolls.

Whitney knew little about growing cotton. But legend says that he designed his first model in just 10 days. That model didn't work, however, because the sticky fiber caught on the teeth of the wooden comb that went through the cotton. Many historians think that Catherine Littlefield Greene suggested that he use wire bristles, like those on her fireplace brush. Her idea worked.

The Fight to Keep the Patent

Catherine Greene suggested to Whitney that he show the device to other people. Copies of Whitney's cotton gin soon began to be used on neighboring plantations. Whitney and Miller had a **patent** on their cotton gin, but farmers did not want to pay fees to use their machine. Catherine Greene invested a lot of money to prove that the cotton gin of Whitney and Miller was the original, not just a copy.

Heavy machinery now does most of the work of baling cotton.

For more than 10 years, the battle was fought in the courts. During the long court battle, Catherine Greene married Phineas Miller. They sold their home to pay the court costs and they moved to a smaller house on their estate. Finally, Whitney was granted clear patent, but it was too late to make any money from the cotton gin. The period of the patent was almost over, and there were many copies around.

Catherine Greene Miller died in 1814 of a fever.

What Was Her Part?

No one knows the full story of the invention of the cotton gin, an important event in the history of the South, slavery, and the Civil War. Tales of Catherine Greene's work on the cotton gin continue to be told. She may have suggested to Whitney how to make the cotton gin. Catherine received some payment for the invention. This might be because she helped invent it. Or, it may have been repayment for money she lent to Whitney.

People who believe that Catherine Greene really invented the cotton gin also think that she was a woman of her time and probably would not have dreamed of putting her own name–a woman's name–on an invention. We may never know just how important Catherine Greene's role was.

Madame C.J. Walker
1867-1919
The Woman Who Invented Herself

The Civil War had been over for only three years when Sarah Breedlove, later known as Madame C.J. Walker, was born. Through her own inventiveness, this daughter of slaves went on to become one of the most important women in the history of the United States.

Sarah Breedlove was born in 1867 in a shack along the Mississippi River in Louisiana. Even though her parents were no longer slaves, they still did the backbreaking labor of tending cotton fields. As a small child, she, too, worked in the fields from the time the sun rose until it set.

When Sarah was seven, her parents died and she went to live with her older sister. The sister's husband was cruel, and Sarah left as soon as she could, to marry at age 14. Several years later, Sarah's husband was killed, leaving Sarah alone with a tiny daughter.

Sarah knew there must be more to life than the pain she had found so far. She moved to St. Louis, Missouri. At first she found work only as a cook.

Things changed for Sarah after she lost her hair. The hair of African-American people ofen curls very tightly. African-American women sometimes used painful methods to straighten their hair. This often made it fall out. Sarah developed a chemical that made the hair grow back again.

Her friends used Sarah's formula, and others began to buy it from her. In 1904, at the age of 37, her only wealth consisted of one dollar and fifty cents. But she took a chance and went into the business of making and selling hair care products for African-American women.

Sarah moved to Denver, Colorado. Her daughter and some other relatives helped her mix and bottle the products. Her new husband, the newspaperman Charles J. Walker, helped her advertise and sell her products by mail. She later divorced Walker, but she kept his name and became known to history as Madame C. J. Walker.

A Woman of Business

As important as her invention of the hair preparation was, even more important was her development of a huge business. She hired

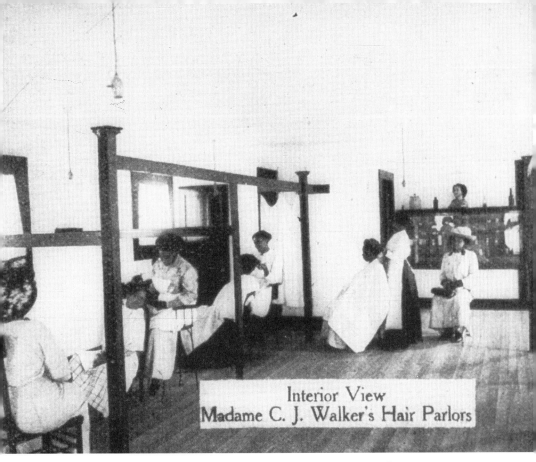

Interior View
Madame C. J. Walker's Hair Parlors

Madame Walker founded a chain of shops where customers could try her hair products.

other African-American women to go door-to-door selling beauty products, just as Avon sales representatives would do at a later date.

She didn't just sell products, however–she sold the Walker Method. The Walker Method consisted of shampoos, conditioners to help

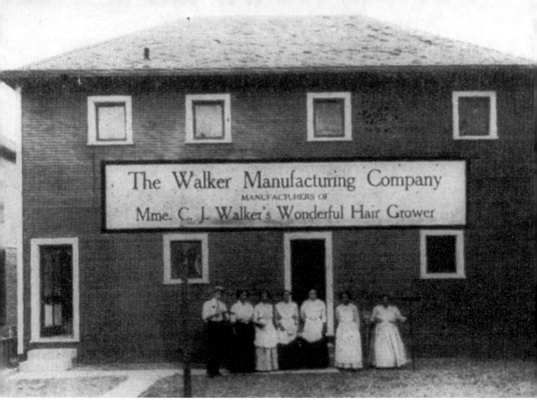

Workers pose outside Madame C. J. Walker's company headquarters.

hair grow, straighteners, and special brushes and combs. Madame Walker developed a special hot comb that made the chemicals work better. The Walker Method produced the smooth, shining, easy-to-manage hair many African-American women wanted.

After a few years in Denver, Madame Walker and her daughter moved to Pittsburgh, Pennsylvania, to open a beauty college to train African-American women in her methods. She later settled in Indianapolis, Indiana, where her company's headquarters were to remain for the rest of her life.

Walker opened beauty salons across America, wherever large groups of African Americans were to be found. She also expanded into South America. Thousands of

Madame Walker Giving a Manicure

black women sold her products. They discovered for themselves the pleasure of being in business instead of working only as servants.

Other black women became inventors because of Sarah Walker. Marjorie Joyner, of Indianapolis, for example, was an employee of Madame Walker's who earned a patent for a permanent wave machine in 1928.

Madame Walker became the first American woman to become a millionaire by her own efforts. She always remembered the cotton fields from which she came. Because she did not learn to read and write until long after her business was successful, she strongly supported education for blacks. She encouraged African-American women to vote. Most of all, she gave other black women hope that they, too, could move beyond their humble beginnings.

Harriet Hosmer
1830-1908
Artist and Inventor

Harriet Hosmer was an artist who had many original ideas. She was the first famous American woman sculptor. She was also an inventor.

Harriet Goodhue Hosmer was born in Watertown, Massachusetts, in 1830. Her father taught Harriet, his only child, all the things he might have taught a son. He encouraged her to solve problems and to invent ways to simplify household tasks.

As a teenager living in St. Louis, Missouri, Harriet loved art. She decided to be a sculptor, to make beautiful statues. She knew that she needed to learn about the human body in order to sculpt the human figure well. At that time, however, it was not easy–even for a male medical student–to study **anatomy**. It was nearly impossible for a young woman artist.

Her father persuaded a physician in St. Louis to teach her about anatomy. When people found out, they were horrified that a young woman would want to learn about the human body.

Harriet Hosmer's statue of Thomas Hart Benton brought her worldwide recognition.

In Hosmer's time, nobody believed a woman capable of creating a monumental statue.

Surely Not a Woman

In 1852, Harriet went to Rome, Italy. She studied and worked in Rome for many years. She sculpted many statues and busts of famous people. She became the first American woman to gain worldwide fame as a sculptor.

Hosmer's statue of Missouri Senator Thomas Hart Benton was erected in St. Louis. It was said at the time that "Americans may now boast of possessing what no nation in Europe possesses–a public statue by a woman."

Many people did not believe Benton's statue was actually the work of a woman. At America's 100th anniversary celebration in Philadelphia in 1876, Harriet Hosmer was recognized as a famous sculptor. Many people at the time said that surely those wonderful statues could only have been done by a man.

Inventing Fake Marble

By 1879, Hosmer had pretty well given up sculpting. But she was still interested in the materials used for statues, usually marble. Real marble was quite expensive, so she wanted to create an artificial, or fake, marble that could be used by sculptors.

Marble is a very hard kind of **limestone**. It has been formed by higher temperatures and greater pressure than regular limestone. It is

Workmen surround Harriet Hosmer in her studio.

found in many different colors and it can be
polished to a shine.

Harriet made her artificial marble by putting
regular limestone in very hot water under high
pressure. She added dyes to create the colors
that nature would give to real marble. Hosmer
had her lawyer secretly patent the invention,
which she called petrified marble. This fake

marble worked well as decoration for the interiors of buildings, where its shine and color looked like marble. Many builders used Hosmer's fake marble in the coming decades. But her process did not produce stone of good enough quality for sculptors.

Later in her life, Hosmer tried to invent a **perpetual motion** machine. Such a machine is probably not possible. Any machine that moves

Marble is a hard limestone that is used by sculptors to create statues.

has to have new energy put into it in order to keep moving. Otherwise, it slows down and eventually stops. She made many designs for a machine that would overcome this problem. Nothing was ever patented.

Hosmer used magnets in her work on the perpetual motion machine. This led her to invent a magnetic motor that was regarded as very important. She patented it in England.

Toward the end of her life, Harriet Hosmer briefly returned to **sculpture**. She created the statue of Queen Isabella of Spain shown at the 1892 World's Fair in Chicago. Altogether, Harriet Hosmer probably had at least five patents and perhaps as many as seven.

Yvonne Brill
1924-
Inventor for the Future

Yvonne Brill was in the right place at the right time to study rockets and to help form America's space program. Her rockets were not the giant ones that hurled men and women into space. But they are just as important.

Brill's tiny, electric-powered rockets are used to position **communications satellites** in their **orbits**. We rely on these satellites for worldwide telephone service, for long-range television broadcasts that reach across the oceans, and even for local cable television from a neighboring city.

Student, Wife, Mother, and Engineer

Yvonne Claeys Brill was born in 1924 in the province of Manitoba, in Canada. She received her degree in chemistry from the University of Manitoba and, later, another degree from the University of Southern California.

When World War II was ending, Brill went to work for an aircraft manufacturer as a mathematician. Then, in the late 1940s, when most people had not even heard of rockets except as German weapons of war, Brill began to work on the future. She studied rocket **propellants**, or fuel, and rocket **propulsion** systems–rocket engines and controls.

After interrupting her work to raise three children, Yvonne returned to the RCA Corporation in 1964. The company was then developing rocket propulsion on a small scale. They needed small rocket systems that could maneuver satellites already in orbit. In addition, RCA was a major maker of communications satellites, which are positioned in an orbit 22,300 miles (35,680 kilometers) above the earth.

Brill's Electrical Rocket

Yvonne Brill concentrated on electrical propulsion. Using a chemical called **hydrazine**, she invented and patented the hydrazine/hydrazine resistojet system. This system works by electrically heating the fuel in the satellite's rockets. This makes the fuel work more efficiently. Less fuel is needed to perform maneuvers. As a result, the satellite has a longer useful life.

Brill's system was patented in 1974. Within 10 years, the RCA company was using it on new communications satellites. The system allowed a satellite to carry into space a smaller load of fuel or a larger load of instruments. Brill also developed standards to measure the performance of various rocket fuels. For her work, *Harper's Bazaar* magazine and DeBeers Corporation awarded Yvonne the Diamond Superwoman Award.

Later, Yvonne Brill went to London, England, to work with the International Maritime Satellite Corporation. She is still an adviser to the U.S. Air Force on scientific matters.

Nancy Perkins
1949-
Designer for Industry

Many patents are granted for new designs of existing devices. The people who work on these new designs are called industrial designers.

Nancy Perkins is an industrial designer who has been designing equipment that is easily used by all people. She wants the equipment she designs to be practical as well as attractive.

Designing for People

Nancy Perkins learned about inventing from her family. Her great-aunt, Anna Keichline, an architect, was an inventor who designed building construction methods and furniture.

Nancy wanted to follow in her great-aunt's footsteps. She studied industrial design at the

University of Illinois. When she finished college, it was not easy to find a job, because there were so few women industrial designers. Hired by Sears, Roebuck and Company in 1979, Nancy Perkins was given the task of redesigning the best vacuum cleaner Sears sold.

Perkins thinks she approached the problem differently than a man might. She regards her job as designing for people, not just for industry. She wants the products she designs to be used easily and comfortably by people. She thinks that male designers may not consider how heavy a vacuum cleaner is or how easily it can be moved. She received a patent for her design of a nozzle and container on the Sears vacuum cleaner that made it lighter and easier to move.

In designing a dishwasher, Perkins clearly marked the controls and placed them in the proper order. Even someone who does not read English can understand them.

Getting Out of the Kitchen

Nancy Perkins fought to be assigned to non-female items. She did not want to be thought of only as a designer of household products for women. She was eventually granted another patent for her design of a Sears Die-Hard battery called the IncrediCell. She also designed equipment to be used to test cars automatically when they are brought in for a tuneup. In 1984, Nancy Perkins won the Sears Innovation of the Year Award for her work.

Before starting to design something, Perkins meets with many small groups of people. She talks with them about how they use the item. What do they like about it? What do they dislike about it? What is important to them in buying and using it? These groups help her decide the best way to approach a problem.

Nancy Perkins has started her own industrial design business, Perkins Design Ltd., in Chicago. In her own business, she has designed such products as a fiberglass boat and a small makeup case that lights up.

NO MODEL.

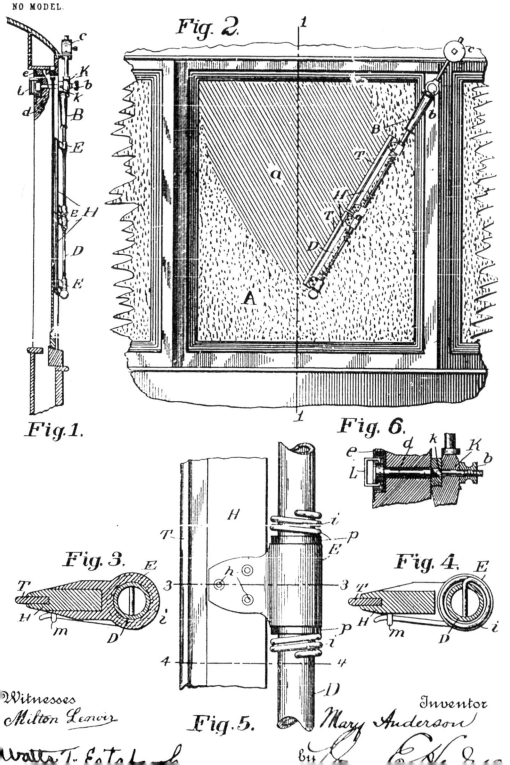

Fig. 2.

Fig. 1.

Fig. 6.

Fig. 3.

Fig. 5.

Fig. 4.

Witnesses
Milton Lenoir
Watts T. Estabrook

Inventor
Mary Anderson

More about Inventing

If you have a good idea for a product, you don't want anyone to copy it. To prevent copying, you need a patent from the government. A patent says that your product is original and useful. Most important, it says that no one can make something just like it without paying you for the right to do so.

To be granted a patent, your invention must be original and useful. There are also some things it cannot be. It cannot just be a way of doing something, and it cannot be just an improvement on an older device. Also, it

This patent drawing shows a windshied wiper system invented by Mary Anderson in the early 20th century.

cannot be just written material. A book, for example, is protected by a copyright, not a patent.

What to Do with a Good Idea

You may have a bright idea for a new or improved product. You need to know how it can be produced. You also have to figure out what claims you can make for it. Are all of its parts new? What is it good for? Just how useful is it?

Many people have a lawyer help them find out whether anything about their invention is already protected by another patent. The lawyer can help an inventor file the right papers for a patent. For more information on the details of obtaining a patent, write:

Office of Information
U.S. Patent Office
Washington, D.C. 20231

or:

Canadian Intellectual Property Office
Industry Canada
Place du Portage, Phase I
50 Victoria Street
Hull, Québec K1A 0C9
Canada

Invent America!

The U.S. Patent Model Foundation is trying to find and preserve models of patented items made in the 19th century. They are also trying to make sure that Americans invent new things in the 21st century.

Invent America! is a program to encourage elementary school students to think creatively. Each year since 1984, students have submitted their inventions. They go to Washington, D.C., to vie for prizes in a national competition.

Some of the inventions created by elementary school children are unusual. One is pet food served with an edible spoon, so the pet owner does not have to wash the spoon. Another is a disposable shield to protect a painter's hand from a drippy paint brush. A third is a floating jigsaw puzzle to play in a pool or in the bathtub.

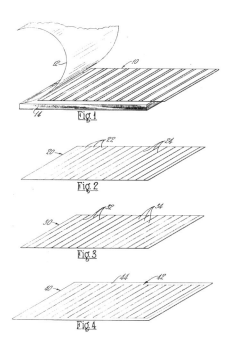

Becky Schroeder's Glo-Sheet, which shines in the dark, allows the user to write straight lines with no light.

Glossary

anatomy–the study of the details of the human body

boll–the fruit of the cotton plant, which holds the seeds that must be taken out before the cotton can be processed

communications satellite–a satellite launched from earth into an orbit 22,300 miles (35,680 kilometers) up, where it remains in place over a certain spot on the earth

hydrazine–a colorless, smoking chemical

limestone–rock formed out of the shells of ancient sea animals, such as coral

orbit–the path an object or natural body follows through space

patent–a government ruling that states a certain device was created by a certain individual

perpetual motion–the idea that a machine can be made that will run forever, without energy being added from outside sources

propellants–rocket fuels

propulsion–the system that moves a rocket in space. It must contain both a fuel and an oxygen source.

sculpture–art in three dimensions, often human figures. A person who makes sculpture is known as a sculptor.

To Learn More

Aaseng, Nathan. *Twentieth-Century Inventors*. New York: Facts on File, 1991.

Bundles, A'Lelia Perry. *Madam C.J. Walker.* New York: Chelsea House Publishers, 1991.

Epstein, Vivian Sheldon. *History of Women in Science for Young People*. Denver, Colo.: VSE Publishers, 1994.

James, Portia P. *The Real McCoy: African-American Invention and Innovation, 1619-1930*. Washington, D.C.: Smithsonian Institution, 1989.

Lafferty, Peter. *The Inventor Through History.* New York: Thompson Learning, 1993.

Macaulay, David. *The Way Things Work*. Boston: Houghton Mifflin, 1988.

McKissack, Patricia and McKissack, Fredrick. *African-American Inventors.* Brookfield, Conn.: The Millbrook Press, 1994.

Pizer, Vernon. *Shortchanged by History: America's Neglected Innovators.* New York: Putnam, 1979.

Richardson, Robert O. *The Weird and Wondrous World of Patents.* New York: Sterling Publishing, 1990.

Showell, Ellen and Amram, Fred M.B. *From Indian Corn to Outer Space: Women Invent in America.* Peterborough, N.H.: Cobblestone Publishing, 1995.

Sproule, Anna. *New Ideas in Industry: Women History Makers.* New York: Hampstead Press, 1988.

Vare, Ethlie Ann and Ptacek, Greg. *Women Inventors and Their Discoveries.* Minneapolis: The Oliver Press, 1993.

Veglahn, Nancy. *Women Scientists.* New York: Facts on File, 1991.

Weiss, Harvey. *How to be an Inventor.* New York: Thomas Y. Crowell, 1980.

Yenne, Bill. *100 Inventions That Shaped World History.* San Francisco: Bluewood Books, 1993.

You can read articles about women inventors in the June 1994 issue of *Cobblestone: The History Magazine for Young People.*

Places to Visit

**Inventure Place: National Inventors
  Hall of Fame**
221 S. Broadway
Akron, OH 44308

Alabama Space and Rocket Center
Tranquillity Base
Huntsville, AL 35807

**California Museum of Science and
  Industry**
700 State Drive
Los Angeles, CA 90037

Eli Whitney Museum
945 Whitney Ave.
Hamden, CT 06517

Franklin Institute Science Museum and Planetarium
20th and Benjamin Franklin Parkway
Philadelphia, PA 19103

Museum of Science
Science Park
Boston, MA 02114

Museum of Science and Industry
57th Street and Lake Shore Drive
Chicago, IL 60637

National Air and Space Museum
Sixth and Independence Avenue S.W.
Washington, DC 20560

National Museum of American History
24th Street and Constitution Avenue N.W.
Washington, DC 20560

Some Useful Addresses

Affiliated Inventors Foundation
2132 E. Bijou St.
Colorado Springs, CO 80909-5950

Invent America!
510 King St. Suite 420
Alexandria, VA 22314

Inventors Clubs of America
Box 450261
Atlanta, GA 30345

**Inventors Workshop International
 Education Foundation**
7332 Mason Ave.
Canoga Park, CA 91306

National Inventors Foundation
345 W. Cypress St.
Glendale, CA 91204

National Women's History Project
7738 Bell Road
Windsor, CA 95492

Society of Women Engineers
120 Wall St., 11th Floor
New York, NY 10005

The Women Inventors Project
1 Greensboro Drive, Suite 302
Etobicoke, Ontario M9W 1C8
Canada

A Summer Camp for Young Inventors

Hands-on activities in science, technology, and the arts are offered at Camp Invention, a weeklong summer camp held at various sites throughout the United States. The camps, sponsored by The National Inventors Hall of Fame, are for students in grades one through five. A companion program, Camp Ingenuity, was recently launched for students in grades six through eight. For information, call 1-800-968-4332.

Index

Photo credits: Library of Congress General Collections: pp. 17, 18, 20, 22, 23; Library of Congress Manuscripts Division: pp. 10, 13, 14, 15; Library of Congress Prints & Photo Division: pp. 4, 8; US Patent & Trademark Office: p. 28; p. 25 used with permission of the Society of Women Engineers, New York, NY.